waited too long......

She still
WAITS

DIA AGRAWAL

Welcome!

SO... ARE YOU READY TO JUMP INTO MY NOVEL POOL which is gonna be full deep with words and emotions and it's not only my words but also it's a desire of all women across the world who want changes in their home, in their lifestyle and in their inner soul. THIS NOVEL indicates that

SHE IS WAITING FOR A WORLD , WHERE SHE COULD BE 'I'. THIS BOOK is all about a war that SHE STILL fights with inner self

every single word and coma in book . i typed on the keyboard.

Dia

"how broken the heart , when it thought of its fake death certificate"

S H E   D R E A M S

"she dreams to fly,not to cry.
she dreams to dive,and to drive.
she dreams a life that she drew
not
that people had painted for her.

But
That Dreadful DarkNight,
'her dreams got shred'
'just like my t i t l e'

and now she dreams that
'she used to dream'

THE GOOD THING IS-
~"SHE STILL DREAMS."~

"it's okay when dreams got crumbled
but it shattered now"

a walk to remember

"she walks normally.
she can feel her footsteps.
she saw shadow on road but not hers.
she walks fast.
but the distance between
hers and that shadow
 remain same.
so NOW
she runs.
but
both shadow got met.
she walks normally again.
BUT IN HEAVEN."

"so many, to kiss your lips,
but any? , to kiss your cuts!.

kiss your lips show love ,
but
kissing the cuts show healing that love."

"To make you feel insecure
is to confess
A vacant place in heart."

"if nothing goes in your favor
then Be Blessed
because a great thing is in search of you ."

"Grateful to have the bunches of worst phases because
I'm getting the best temporary faces as a gift."

" everyone said ,"look ! moon is half."
but she saw,
incomplete isn't moon ,its shine is"

~dia

AND SHE STILL WAITS !

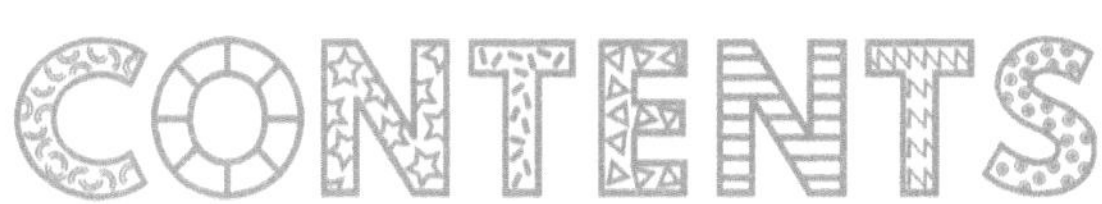

CONTENTS

CHAPTER ONE

A NIGHTMARE

A dark blank black spot around me, that i can't see any light and suddenly a sound stroke me --oh my mother woke me up, every morning she disturbs me for school. it's not like that i hate school , i love school but only for *friends.*

we are known as *Monsters of our School.* we had shook our school on our four hands . one hand is *nacy* ,second is *rile*,third is *uvi* and the last but not the least *ishy.* oops my mother came with a glass of milk into my room again to wake me up.

until she'll come i already made my bed like a good girl but can't understand why my friends considered me a bad bitch and my family also thinks that all bad things happen because of my fault.leave it I'm getting late for my school.

"OH MAN CAN'T YOU SEE ? YOU HIT MY SCOOTER.....THESE FUCKING HEAVY DRIVERS !!!!"

i just stepping towards my class after had my longest breakfast with parents who gave me illogical lectures about my using too much phone and being social all the time . For them i am on my phone all day and night but there is a reality check that i use it for a short time frequently.

And in all that mess the sad part is my phone got scratches because of that B*LOODY HEAVY DRIVER!*

"MAY I COME IN MA'AM?" I ASKED
the three faces look at me with a smile and tensed face because i am too late
for the class and all thanks to that fucking driver but maybe nobody hit her
scooter that's why she is in good mood so she said nothing to me except
-- sit on your seat quickly --   otherwise she finds an opportunity to scold me.

uvi asked "why are you so late?" i just take a deep breathe and telling all the mess to them ,

without interval i take a break in my storytelling because ma'am is staring at us through her specs with deep angry eyes. for a moment we think maybe that's why we called
"Monsters of the School."

our hands are tired hanging on air upward for last ten minutes. yes we got punished but who the hell out of us who do the same as mam told, we ran far from that punish place and moving towards our *favorite spot*

---backyard of school--

we used to spend our lots of wastage hours and hours here. this is our *bunking spot* because no one checks here
and, like always we gossip and make fun of each other, i and rile always automatically team up by itself and roast the rests.

"we're too close, only in a friendship manner."

my parents know my friends group except rile .yes as i born in strict family i kept telling all my school stuff in which only females are character.my mom knows rile as just only my classmate with whom i talk only to borrow some pens and that's all ~.

"for dad there is no boy exist in my entire universe"

after roasting session we stepped out of the school and go to our second *favorite spot* ---our special chai tapri---a small wood type tea stall and here is *our most favorite thing of us* after seventh bell to take a sip of tea after rolling into these damn frustrated-irritated classes .

These spots are my favorite but not that dream one that i
saw in my morning ,that one is just like that my future
career is going to finish and only to think about that

i feel null
i don't even love my parents who gave birth to me
as much as i love my career.....

~ and after this statement - i feel null again.!

with that we take a sip and judge those who got noticed from
our intense eyes and a women is caught but not from our,
only from ~my eyes~

SHE is driving her own car by itself and having fun with her
friends in car .
the laugh , the fun, the joy i hear , i
see, i observe but said nothing because all this belongs to her
not me. I'm
not being jealous but i also want that freedom, that
modernness , that independency , that attitude so i too can
take my friends on a
trip on by myself and there we'll gonna do so much fun.

"I want my life craziest and wildest with full of adventurous that there will no time left to be upset."

give you guys a reality check my life is totally different than my imaginations.....

now it's 5 pm and time to go home .let's see what's different in snacks today! otherwise mom only used to bake that same boring calzone.

I parked the scooter in my garage and move towards the mom with a little bit hope that gets some happiness but *Wait what* there is no chef ,my happiness has gone for supermarket.

I think that's the double happiness that i can cook my food by myself but that type of independency i don't expect or wish from GOD.

okay so let's make cheese burger, ~ahaa!! that's my all time favorite dish that i can eat even when i am sleeping.

i just wore my apron only then my sadness knock with the stuff that bring from the supermarket.

she said "oh dear you came .now go and wash your hands. calzone is waiting for you . let me bring it from the fridge"

"wow ,she already bake that fucking calzone" i muttered in my mind.

Chapter Two

Neighbor's Night out

After having dinner ,laying on my bed in my own privacy room hits different . i feel another level of calmness and peace that the day goes off and i have full night with myself .there will be no one to interrupt me but i was wrong .

"OH GOD! WHY I SEE THIS...WHY!!!!"
I screamed staring at roof of my room.
(that's my way talkING to the GOD)

through my window unintentionally my eyes caught a moment of silent violence yes you read right
--a silent violence--

my neighbor aunt sushi is going for a dinner with her husband. uncle put the key in and the car starts and within a couple of minutes they flew away like a wave of wind.

There is an dark peaceful empty road left for me to watch. now pick my phone and start to check my social media.
again there is a interruption ,seems like someone park its car   -oh aunt came back.

i saw the time on my phone thinking how fast two hours passed. now i avoid these interruptions and focus on my 'me time' .

my eyes caught aunt sitting on a window and staring at the moon with a drop of tear in her eyes seems like if she close her eyes then this drop fell down on her cheeks. on the other hand uncle is snoring ~loudly~.

To see them as a couple, i thought-

" Husbands has a remote control of their wives that they will do every work according to their hubby's will."

They can't eat until their husband don't .
They can't walk ahead of their husband .

"SHE CAN'T BE MORE SUCCESSFUL THAN HER HUSBAND."

"SHE CAN DO WORK HARD BUT NOT AS MUCH THAT MAKE HER MORE SUCCESSFUL THAN HER HUBBY ."

if she does it then she is not a good wife , not a good daughter-in-law and overall not a good creature. she is worthless. she only wants luxury lifestyle not goodness of her husband and her in laws who always stand far where she need and want their support the most.

"TILL NOW IN MOST OF THE FAMILIES SHE WORKS LIKE A LABOR EVEN DURING HER PREGNANCY TIME"

(SHE REFERS TO WOMEN ALL OVER THE WORLD)

i know why my aunt is sad and went for a dinner date but i am unable to do anything for her because i'm just 15 and i have no money that i can handle all her expenses by myself and dad won't give me a single coin.

i just love when she said, "Ishy come!, I just made your favorite cheese burger..!!" and that's the only noise that i like from her house,

or else every time when i thought about that horrible terrifying night 'my hands still shudder'.

those screams , cry out in pain, frightened and pale face,
her face is filled with too much sweating mixed with tears,
begging with her red- teary eyes
(her eye veins is clearly noticeable)
begging every moment that she don't miss any moment to beg.

but alcoholic uncle, in his full mood to release his complete frustration of work on that roadside beggar ~(aunt)~.

she gave her hundred percent to get free from the grip of his hands that holding her hair tightly and right in front of my eyes,seeing the sight through my room's window, he drag aunt away across the floor,

maybe in another room to beat her with the belt because seems like uncle didn't done yet or he is not enjoying ,only with hands, he wants more scars on her body .

"A MAN CAN NEVER SEE HIS WIFE TO BE MORE SUCCESSFUL THAN HIM BUT HE CAN SEE MORE SCARS ON HER THAN HIMSELF."

now after beating session, there is a ritual held in their house for past four years to go on a dinner date as a compensation and next day, they happily went for a date

and just like that aunt went for so many dates with her hubby ,but before last four years she won't go for a date,maybe because she lived with her mom.

and once i noticed they had gone for a date five times in a week. "leave it man! let's check my social media" i said along with releasing my breathe.

" after two hours i couldn't check" i muttered .

i don't know why my mind force me to think about that incident in which aunt got *miscarriage*.

'yes she went for a dinner date even during her pregnancy.'

''how can someone be so heartless that kick his own wife's belly with its sharp cut shoe's heel

when she is 'six months pregnant'.

"oh my god!!!! how much pain she bore at that time , at that moment."

if i was at her place then definitely lodge an FIR,

'' but aunt sushi is still eating delicious food on her dinner date with her baby killer.''

Chapter Three

GET TOGETHER PARTY

"damn yr, my mom again come with a glass of milk into my room, maybe its her ritual to treat me so that i shut my mouth up whenever she scold me

but that's not delicious man!!!" i murmured.

 i have to reach school on a time because god knows how's the ma'am mood today.? i think sh'll be on her periods all the time as she has too much mood swings.

"may i come in ma'am?" i take permission.

i am fully surprised that why is she smiling and said with a soft tone voice, "come child! have a seat.."
i sat down beside rile and asked , "what's happening? dude.."

he said, "nothing bro,it's just her last class with us so she got some sentiments"

"oh i see......" i replied

"i forgot about my upcoming exams. and then we all move to different-different colleges. this is the last time we sit together on benches in our uniform , having no tension about career,about how to earn money otherwise

"we will all get lost in the crowd of earners."

I think i got more sentiments rather than ma'am and not only ma'am but also i too have last class with my fellow mates" i said in my mind.

"now seventh bell rings and school is over in no time"

we went for our sipping session as it's our ritual after school ends and making fun of those who got caught . in between nacy become senti and her voice is weeping

and because of her we also filled with sentiments and recall all our happy faces and moments that we spent together and especially those gossips which we had done in backyard.

suddenly rile stand up and announced with a cheerful voice that we should throw a GET TOGETHER PARTY after exams.
we were get so- so much excited to hear this that we make our own plans already in our mind that what dress should i wore? which theme should we select and so on.......

but there is a question that strike in my mind that how can i say to my parents that rile , 'a boy' , come over to that same party which he organizes.

"excited rile sat down on the stool and my worry stands up"

'leave it! let's see after exams ,which excuse will work....' i set up in my mind.

"oh! this question...i think i read it in the morning",i think someone is looking at me , turn, oh god this uvi -she really don't know any cheating tricks ,why she staring at me like that in front of the teacher .

if ma'am saw then we will gonna be finish. i turn toward nacy and with my cheating experience i give signs to her to take care of that uvi otherwise on the last day of exam we will get stuck in a trap because of her.

bell rings, teacher start to collect copies from students. in the last only we four are left in class as ma'am ordered. we were scared that now what had we done .she come towards us with no clue that what she is going to do and then she gives us chocolate from her pink purse .

that time we thought that till now we got only one advantage of being and called
'Monsters of the School'

rile said with excitement with a loud voice, "oh yeah!!! finally the exams is over.....NOW IT'S TIME TO PARTY!!!!!!!!!!
every girl become excited except me because i know my roots that never said 'yes' to me.
uvi noticed my worry face that is hidden behind my smiley face.she moved towards me and said with lower voice, "what happened ishy? you don't look happy"

i just can't understand that how got she know ,when i give my best to hide that worry .

"i think that's the real friends do!"

i shared all my tension that twirling around my head to nacy and uvi and within seconds i feel so much relaxed that hundred of tons burden got vanished on my head.

"Both are like a home to me , a sweet happy home where worry and sadness can't knock"

it feels if i couldn't attend the party then it's okay because i have these gems beside my side always .

"the ones who support me even if all fault will be mine."

they give me idea that there is no need to tell your parents about any boy because in their eyes boys aren't allowed because you tell them that it's a Girls Party...

" sounds interesting but what if they got know about our plan from someone....?" i asked curiously.

"oh god.....trust me ishy nothing will be happen." nacy said with humbleness.

"i just feel, one blind is following another blind.."

with a glass of beer, i sat down on the stool of bar in the streets of colombia. my friends are dancing and crying hard seems they got set for the night.

they give signals again and again to me to hit the dance floor with them but i'm not in a mood maybe because of my parents that they don't get know about the boys .

''but i keep them aside and with a long breathe i drink the beer and ran for the dance. dancing with these crack ones are my most favorite thing. i dance too much.i enjoy too much.now my body is full sweating .

i have to go to beer counter again .i'm not alcoholic, i just drink occasionally and my parents only know about soft drinks habits.

''turn back because someone holds my hand oh that's rile .seems he wants to dance with me. he said with a smile , "Not with me, girl!"

how can i refuse to my best friend so we danced together. we set a fire on the dance floor.

"it was so much fun to dance with you,buddy" i said with my low breathe .

''now i have to go to take some beer or else i'm gonna die on that floor.

when we take our second sip together, yudi(one of my
classmate) came over and showing dancing pictures of me and
rile together which he clicked without permission .rile told
him to send these pics to us and then uvi and nacy also join us

and for last three hours we were gossiping
about our 'us' moments nonstop and for my parents i'm
enjoying at uvi's place.

''i literally feel like that independent
women who was enjoying with her friends in her own car. here i
feel that

'' i stay more happy with these crack ones rather than my
family.
"and just like school , night is over too."

i press the switch and bell rings, of my home,mom opened the
door and said, " you should have come a little late" ,
with a taunt voice.

i went for take a shower and in that time i
don't know what changes happen with my parents . they were
angry in such a way like today is my last day on earth. then i
noticed my phone in my mom's hand .probably she saw my
dancing pictures with rile as yudi send it. i become helpless
and pale just like aunt sushi . i thought they are going to do
the same with me as uncle did to aunt.

''dad looks like he will eat me without pepper and salt.''

in full argument session, there is no words that i utter, seems someone switch on my mute button.

i'm just waiting when will this get over, the only thing i pray to get over 'after night and school'

''but i am shattered at the ending as my dad announced in his house that ishy is not going anywhere. from now,she'll be at home.

and where i shattered - "and her admission in college of L.A. will be cancelled"

"if staying with us she is doing that rubbish thing with boys then there ,without us she probably got pregnant"
his words is just like a sharp cut knife that goes straight to my heart.

two days passed , but there is no hope left that take me to L.A.

my phone rings , i got annoyed because all, 'because of it'!!!!!

but i got happy to see urvi name on it -oh that's her call , here i got some hope .

but there is a mystery that i can't understand that when my father said those sharp cutting words, i observed my mother's sad face ,seems she is not happy with what's happening with me.~

Chapter Four

My MOM'S MOTHERS

"that's not a get together party , that's a life changing party for me.... urvi! i really can't understand what should i do...i can't live in this hell through my life.

    ' please man! just kidnap me from my dad's house.'

-oh! my mom is coming.....call you back later!!!!!!"
cut the call ,throwing it on my bed. sitting on a chair with my two second expression changed face that convert into a sad face that about to cry.
 a soft tone voice came from outside the door, a voice that want to heal me and then my mom entered into my room by saying,

        "Don't worry my dear, i will help you to get out of this shit."
i was just surprised that "is she my mom or what....."
       ''but finally i got hope in my own dad's house in the form of his wife

i'm wondering that why does she want to help me. Is she want something from me but i don't have anything that i can give her, already she has a lot. now she is heading outside the room.

     ''maybe she is a housewife that's why she thought of not putting me into this profession because everyone hates their job and especially the BOSS. her boss is my grandma. my mom always used to consider my grandma 'DRAGON OF THE HOUSE' but in same manner she is right because my grandma never miss a chance to interfere in my mom's work. when she made a dessert, everyone like it except boss, ''saying, 'lack of sugar in it' .

"she bear her boss's nonstop taunt all the time, all day, everyday without any complain."

"she even don't take any leave from the day when she joins."

"she just want some love and peace from her mother-in-law but she get hate and taunts as a gift."

grandma always wanted a well educated girl for his loving son but 'she got my innocent sweet mom as a blessing from GOD.'

she even managed all household chores by herself during pregnancy in which 'cleaning and cooking is the basic needs of human' but there is no mistake of my family members because they aren't human in my dictionary.

i remember when my mom is talking on a call and said with a replied tone, "they don't want me, they just want gifts from my dad."

"if they want gifts then they can buy from the store. why they make my mom life hell....?" - i opinioned.

"they buy my mom with no money and along with grab gifts from her family."

My Mom don't share these ''trauma giving incidents' to her biological mother because she is disappointed that her mother never take a stand for her .

''whenever she needs her support the most, a expressionless face she got.

'at the age of playing with friends, she kept busy with nani's household chores. she handled all by herself
and at the age of going L.A. for further studies , she got selled to my dad

but one thing my dad's family confirmed-
" is she capable to be our servant or not..?"~

"she dreams of being her best version to them and they went out of the house to seek for a modern housemaid"

'and the deal got done!'

with the deal, she also get done with her shattered dreams and all credit goes to my mom's mother and her expressionless face.

"it's okay when her dreams got crumbled but it shattered now."

if she studied with focus then her mother yell , "what are you rubbish doing...at last you have to do that same bullshit, that I'm doing since i born......"

    ''SHE probably met two Dragons in her whole life,

   one who is dying thinking that my mom wants to grab their rude son from them
    and the special other one who let that rude family give rights to ruin their own daughter's life.

   "I'm blessed that having a 'mom' otherwise
  mom just met two mothers through her whole life"

i think it's correct time to talk to urvi as my mom has gone out for supermarket.

MAY IT HAPPEN! she would come back with a cheeseburger...

Chapter Five

HOW TO SWIM

"oh god! nacy...I'm done with my family.they don't
understand me . they just want to get their 'so called ego' win
but in thousand wrongs there is one right thing that my
grandma went to her husband's place forever in heaven." -

i said within a single breathe.
then urvi asked, "that means you have only one option -
!!!!"MARRIAGE" !!!!
there, you can continue your studies.."
nacy solaced me that, " don't listen to
her, you just relaxed and keep trying and overall ,
aunt is with you baby!"
and the conference call ends.!

but urvi's words are going on my mind because it hits me hard
as i overhear my dad's words to mom that, " in two years i'll
get your characterless daughter married , i have some respect
in a society, i'll not let your daughter ruin it."

and with that i got crumbled on the floor.
my face get filled with sweat within a second and directly
move towards the terrace --my third most loving favorite spot
of dad's house-- .

'' lack of oxygen in my lungs,!!
,got an idea to escape from this 'dream killer house' but don't
have money even to buy my cheeseburgers.

"without marriage,my life seems not more than hell but after marriage it will definitely look like a hell surrounded with devils"

'at this time at least i have my mom, after dealing i'll have no one who will support me in my further studies. i think history repeats, 'at the age of going L.A. ,
I am transferring to jail that is called by 'my home'.

because dad's house is not my home because i don't belong to them.
"i am just born to be a burden on them."

"but there is a fun fact that MY Home's residents believe, a MODERN HOUSEMAID is coming to join their happy family 'and they will avail of her full'."~

unfortunately, this house is known as her husband's place.
then
~ <u>where's her home</u>?
before marriage i lived my life on my father's terms and conditions and after *transportation* i'm living on my hubby's terms.
then
~ <u>where the hell are my life!!, my terms..!?</u> ~

i think god has divided my life into two section-
'first section holder are fathers and second section holder are husbands.'

"they feed , they care , they love but don't let her fly."

"she spent her whole life happily,
staying in the grip of shackles."

'ishy was tearing her bucket list page from her diary as it
doesn't matter or 'it never existed'. she wants to see the ash of
that page.'
(*The combination of anger,sadness,helpless made her to do that*) .
but on another side, ishy is hustling to get rid of this trauma
that she got as a gift from her father.

"if he can't make me happy then at
least don't do such things that break me badly."

i think ishy is no more...... 'inside me' , 'a loving crazy fun
girl who always lived with a smiley face.'

"yes lived., because 'live' is no more.!"

but nacy's letters also hit different because maybe 'i can save
myself from my current devil, through his wife.'

"At his devil's stubbornness,
he wants to sink me
where i don't know
how to swim."

Chapter Six

Stranger: A REAL MAN

'bell rings. seems , 'my mom came back from the supermarket
with a cheeseburger. i went straight to open the door for her,

''but i wish that i can also open the door
of happiness for my mom.''

oh my 'MAY IT HAPPEN!' changed into 'HAPPENED IN
REAL'.
she stands on the doorstep holding a cheeseburger in her
hand. it's just like she not only brings a cheeseburger but also
brings a hope,

a light in my 'dark blank nightmare' .

laying on her lap,eating my tasty cheeseburger, my mind got
me lost in another world but my another mind wants to stay in
this world where it feel peace , calm like i forgot about all,
what shit had happened with me for past two days.
but i got lost.

i made up in my mind already that i'll only go for a love
marriage as i'm watching these beautiful pairs since
childhood-

'uncle and aunt sushi' ,
'my mom and grandma's son'.

because
"surrounded by devils, at least have one white doll as a light."

who supports, take a stand for me, have a faith in me, believe
me and most important - ' GIVE RESPECT TO ME'

"A WOMEN CAN LIVE WITHOUT LOVE BUT CAN'T
BREATHE WITHOUT RESPECT"

~"I DON'T WANT ANY HUSBAND IN MY LIFE .
I CRAVE FOR A MAN."~

but my dad got busy in dealing with a stranger whom i don't
see ever through my life.

''and the stranger is giving his best to show
my dad that he is a 'MAN'. and my dad acknowledged that

"THE STRANGER IS TRULY A REAL MAN."
~ 'IN JUST FIRST MEETING'.~

'and the transportation begins!!!!'

my mom drag me in to the real world by 'caress the head as a
sign of love' that make me feel relieved hundred tons from the
hustling that goes in my head.

i asked her , "did you ever fall in love with someone?"

Chapter Seven

NOT SO SECRET DATE

mom got hesitate and act like that she wish, why ,i have my mouth..?if mouth doesn't exist then question won't arise.. she stands up and went to her room as soon as possible, i followed her and caught her ,standing on the balcony and staring at only one spot- road.

''seems like her mind got her lost in another world. i move close to her and said sorry but there is no response that she didn't hear what i said. then i don't know what should i do...so i came back into my room and closed the door

and when the night fall, i don't know, because of my sleepy eyes. someone knocks my door....it's mom.!

she said, "come for dinner!"
and i said nothing.
then she said again, "your dad had gone out of station"
and i said with a cheerful tone , "coming mom!".

i ate an delicious dinner with mom having no conversation about love.

after cleaning utensils, heading towards my room and closed
the door,
but don't do focus on my 'ME Time'. suddenly again, knocks
the door.
"is it you..mom." - i asked knowingly.
she came up to me and sit beside me on the bed.

                        'definitely, she is going to say
something spicy related to that question which is gonna shock
me.

'she take me in her flashback where she was falling for a guy.
and that guy is her first and last boyfriend. she loved him so
much
                        and in my whole family only me and one
of my mom's friend got a chance to get to know about this
love. my mom shares her all secrets with that friend and
sometimes i overheard their interesting conversation and from
there i got to know about the GIFTS concept of my grandma.

"THEY spent many beautiful special moments together.
  they enjoyed each other company so much.
  they made their 'us' moments many times.
  they kept their relationship far from the eyes of world."

                ''my mom assumed that their couple is
perfect couple and better than these nowadays
  'insecure couples'.

and one day, a weak moment developed their hormones HIGH
and make them to kiss
and she felt heaven.~

'their bond became more strong. that
guy threw a party at his farm house and invited all of his
friends.

and you know, what circumstances my mom had
faced while running from her father's house at midnight after
sleeping the whole family
and she made it.

'my mom looked so pretty in her era.
she wore an above knee length short black dress in which she
was looking stunning as much that

"if i was a boy then i'll marry her for sure."~

The guy became statue to see my stunning gorgeous mom and
his male friends astonished to see my mom at first time.

he came close to her and said in a deep low voice into her
ears,
 "are you my girl..!?"

and then she said with a shy smile and sparkling eyes ,
"yes, all yours!!"

they were dancing together and one of his friends came up to them and all of a sudden , the drink got fallen on her legs .

''his friend was scared to see an angry face of her boyfriend but she calmed down him and take him straight to the room where she was washing her legs with water in a washroom.

then she came out of the washroom and seeing his disturb mood , moved close to him and said with a gentle voice, "forget it baby!, it happens."
but he replied nothing.

so she move close to his lips and the distance between their lips is just that they don't get touch only and said with soft low voice,

"wanna be my man...!?"
and he kissed hard ,while they are kissing, his hand slowly slowly move upwards on her back and stop at the zip and now moving the zip downwards but all of a sudden,

she stopped his hands. their nonstop kiss got a full stop . she said with a lovely voice,
"sorry! but i can't do that..."

and he replied with a gentle voice,
" then don't worry..! only I'll do.."

she was trying to get his point but couldn't. i think after getting know his point ,she wants to make fool herself that she is thinking wrong.

"THE GUY whom she loved
is not the same guy
. that
she is seeing on the bed."

"A BLOODY BED CHANGED MY MAN INTO A BOY"

she was trembling too hard that thousand of questions running through her mind but only one question that strike her hard again and again that

'how would she escape ?'

she just can't get the point that
what makes my man change?
THE BED?
OR
THE NIGHT?
OR
MY ABOVE KNEE LENGTH SHORT DRESS?
OR
THAT I'M LOOKING FUCKING STUNNING TODAY!?
OR
MY WORDS..... "YES, ALL YOURS".

someone please help me to get through of it that
~ " what did i say or do that changed my man in a moment..?"

'her boyfriend convert into a stranger within a second.'

'her entire trust , love , feelings got vanished in just one
blink.'

he pushed me on the bed and
removing his clothes as soon as possible.during
this,someone knocked the door. she thought 'god listened to
her'

but she was also sure
that he won't open the door but surprisingly he headed
towards the door to open it and after opening the doors
she got hope that his friends would save her but they gave
a high five to him.

as they closed the door , all things got cleared , that was
their plan to spell the drink on me so that i would come
here.

'they all are in full mood to avail of her fully.'

''her body got sweaty,she is
shivering ,wandering here and there in search of getting out
of the room, panicked eyes, begging every single moment.

he said, "you said right!, that i'm yours
then be mine.
why only mine....
~ my friends also deserve some fun..!!"

'her heart and mind was completely broke at a single moment' now all her hope got vanished , now there is only one thing left for her -

"TO WAIT TILL THE MORNING."

but before morning, in the shade of moon by god's grace, all benefits she craved to get, of her good works,

that her soul wished to GOD every single second in her heart and mind,

she got in the form of two boys as they just opened the 'door of my freedom' to escape.

' they forgot to lock the door as they were excited to do fun with her.'

she ran fast as much as she can, towards the door and escaped.

in front of the GOD, in church, on knee my mom cried out a
lot and lot.

''from the time she stepped in the
church, felt she is in safe zone now
because she was terrified
on going roads alone,
on seeking lift from auto drivers,
on looking random person
and even
on looking FATHER OF THE CHURCH that she accidentally
met outside the church.

she feels that 'in front of the eyes of GOD' anyone can't even
look at her with their 'lusty eyes'.

she said in a hurtful tone,

"thank you for not letting wait , till the morning........."

Chapter Eight

MY GIRL

i got paused to hear all this trauma and only one thing came up in my mind that

"what would have happened to my mom if she had to wait till the morning"

and with that, she ended her incident with a sentence that is ,

"DON'T FIND A MAN FOR YOURSELF ,
LET DESTINY DO ITS WORK."

''now i'm alone in my room with so much thoughts , questions and many more stuff that bound me.
it's a slow night as i looking out through my window but my mind is not looking there, only my eyes do.

opening my laptop on my legs covered with a cozy pink blanket
and my eyes got shine and lips push my cheeks towards eyes

as i see my favorite INFLUENCER video in a suggestions on youtube that she posted few minutes ago.

i never miss any update of her video .
i just love to watch her videos all day all long .

'the way she vlogs ,
the way she talks ,
the way she do drama
in her video to show that she is funny
so that many people follow her.
it's her way of interacting audience.

and the most important thing that attracts me towards her is that -

"SHE IS LIVING A LIFE THAT I DREAM
EVERY DAY,EVERY MOMENT ."

"she ticked my all bucket lists
through her life"

THE adventure , the craziness , the madness with a group of
friends that i want in my life once

'where i'm not anyone's daughter or respect'

"where i'm just me."

and my influencer 'myra' enjoys my '*once*' in her daily life.

''they live together in a flat and now you got to know that how much madness would be there...

TO watching them on a screen , i always thought that why did i not born in her family.

if it happened then,

' i can make more male friends and sharing their silly stuffs with mom and dad,'

'i go to L.A. for further studies without any interruptions.'

'going on trips with friends and there we'll gonna have fun like her group.'

'live independently alone in a flat like a modern bitch'

''and paying my own bills.'

"I wait for a world
where i can be just me."

i always got goosebumps when i see her doing my bucket list things. i got mixed feeling of jealousy and inspiration.

how she enjoys it
and feel grateful and blessed
for every moment she went through.
and every time when she ticked her bucket list,
'a small amount of water filled her eyes.'

'i also want that small amount of water in my eyes.'
and for sure i don't even complain about getting my eyes wet.

''but my dad played a vital role to get my eyes wet with not just small rather than a large amount of water that goes to my cheeks and fall onto my pillow and made my pillow cover wet.

"SOME INCIDENTS MAKE YOUR EYES WET
AND
SOME ACCIDENTS MAKE YOUR PILLOWS WET. "

Chapter Nine

RUNAWAY

WHAT A BEAUTIFUL MORNING IT IS!

without dad, dad's house looks so pleasant and calm like a heaven. i wish that owner won't come back but can't be possible.but till that moment, i avail of this moment completely.

i went straight to my mom and check her out that she is okay or not....?
but she seems normal as she looks daily.

'so i just hug her and that bloody bell ruin this beautiful and calming moment.'

"my father entered into his house with a long smile on his face and a box of sweets in his hand." me and my mom both are dilemma till now. we think that he must have killed owner of this house and came over here ,wearing his skin.

''that duplicate came up to me and said, "congratulation ! you're getting married...just give your mouth a sweet taste with this box."

i looked at his wife with a hopeless eyes and pale face and
said nothing .

                         just ran into my room and locked it.
'i just can't breathe'.
'there is a lack of oxygen'.
'tears are falling onto the floor continuously'.

                               i wet my pillow again.

his wife knocking the door continuously.
                             and i become deaf.

then after some time i put my chin on the wet pillow and
staring at the leaf of a big tree through my window and recall
about the moment

"when my mom's husband was trying to move his
hands under my skirt."

The door knocks again and
                        then i hug my mom tightly and
cried out a lot. and

                 she thought, it's all because of marriage

and the deal begins !

i'm sitting on a stool wearing a beautiful white
gown with lots of makeup on my face and waiting
for my dad who would come to take me for a aisle.

yes, i agreed to the
wedding because i saw no hope in my mom's eyes
that would take a stand for me.

"A NIGHTMARE
that i showed in first page of my life come true."

"a light
i was seeking
that was just
a white paper"

"now i am shattered like my dreams"

"i always wanted a life that i create
not
that my father already had created
or
not
that my mom is living"

but one thing remains same that

"i can dream,
but only in dreams."

but the good thing is -

"SHE STILL DREAMS"

someone knocks the door. it must be MR. UDIT.
but some women are heading towards me ,saying
wow...! what a beauty.....

i'm getting confused that i
already saw her but where...... , i pressured on my
mind.

oh wait! in the car,
chilling with her friends,
that modern independent women!!

after five days of anxiety and depression, maybe i
started again believing in 'light and hope.'
when they are moving forward to door,

' i stopped her with some courage.'

she stops and now we're alone in that room.

first i told her about that day
when i saw her first time and what i felt to see her .

and then i told her about my
whole story that

how did i get here , in this room...

she felt pity on me that how poor i am!

so she suggested me to escape from
here but she don't know that
i already made up my mind for this
but one thing that stopped
me that i can't even buy a cheeseburger if i did this.

without hesitation, i cleared her with my concept of
cheeseburger.

after thinking for so long, she said,

"don't worry, I'll help you financially.....
and emotionally I'm doing right now."

omg!! i can't understand that
how can someone be so sweet as
she is!!!

she even don't know me as much and she is ready to
help a women.on that note i remember,
someone said,
" WOMEN ARE WOMEN'S WORST ENEMIES"

but i think its totally depend on a person not on a
gender.

i wore an red t-shirt, black jeans with white cap and
black goggles,opened hair and black shoes...
~all set for escape~

she is standing on the doorstep so that no one can
enter. and then i called her , she locked the door and

helped me to set a long scarf
that touches the ground and other end , she'll be
holding with her hands but she knotted it with one
wood leg of bed.

now i 'm descending from the first floor's window to
the end of scarf that touches the ground.

                            ''finally i got off.

FROM NOW,
"MY NEW FRESH LIFE BEGINS,
ON THE NEW FRESH PAGE"

'OLD ISHY IS DEAD NOW.'
'WELCOME TO THE NEW ISHY!!!!'

"SHE IS BOLD
SHE IS BRAVE
SHE DON'T BEAR
SHE IS INDEPENDENT
SHE'LL LIVE HER LIFE ON HER TERMS
SHE IS HERSELF"

"SHE DREAMS"

~"NOW A NEW ISHY IS READY TO TACKLE
WORLDLY PROBLEMS BY HERSELF"~

"SHE CAN DREAM
IN REAL WORLD NOW"

"AN ESCAPE TO HER OWN LIFE"

"SHE HAS A DREAM OF
ESCAPING MANY WOMEN TO THEIR OWN LIFE"

'DOESN'T MATTER' THEY ARE
MARRIED OR NOT,
OLD OR NOT,
RICH OR NOT.

AND THE FIRST MEMBER OF HER NGO
FOR 'ESCAPING WOMEN'
WILL BE -

"<u>HER MOM AND AUNT SUSHI</u>"

then i waved to her and said ,
"GOODBYE AND THANKS A LOT DEAR!"

and she replied with a large smile that covers her
full face and with sparkling eyes,

"I THOUGHT RIGHT THAT MY BROTHER DON'T
DESERVE THIS PRETTY GIRL...."

''and with that she turned
back and headed towards the hall,

where old ishy's mom and dad are waiting and all
relatives too.

"WHAT WILL HAPPEN TO NEW ISHY
WHEN SHE'LL REACH AT
HER 'NEW LIFE',
'NEW FACES',
'NEW COLLEGE'
IN 'NEW L.A.' ?"

"will her new life work in her favor?"

but one thing disturbs me still that-

WOULD THAT STRANGER HAS HELPED
HER BROTHER'S RUNAWAY BRIDE
IN NEW CITY?

(she can't buy even a cheeseburger)

"SEE YOU IN NEXT CHAPTER"

INTERVAL

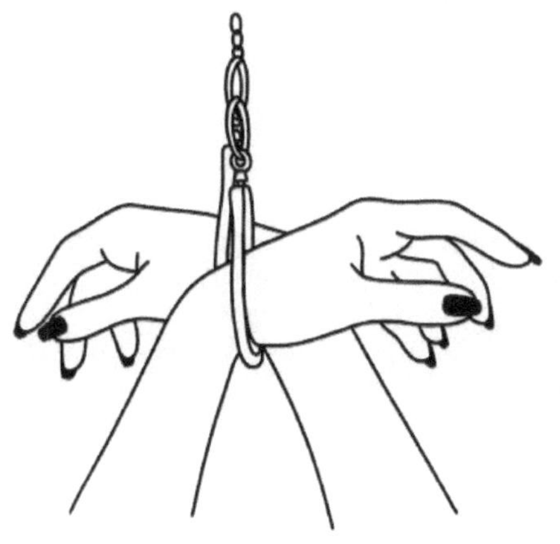

NOT THE END